FEATHER
TALES

Glenda Goose

David M. Sargent, Jr., and his friends live in Northwest Arkansas. His writing career began in 1995 with a cruel joke being played on his mother. The friends pictured with him are (from left to right), Vera, Buffy, and Mary.

Dave Sargent is a lifelong resident of the small town of Prairie Grove, Arkansas. A fourth-generation dairy farmer, Dave began writing in early December, 1990. He enjoys the outdoors and has a real love for birds and animals.

Glenda Goose

By

Dave Sargent

Illustrated by
Jane Lenoir

Ozark Publishing, Inc.
P.O. Box 228
Prairie Grove, AR 72753

Library of Congress cataloging-in-publication data

Sargent, Dave, 1941—
Glenda Goose / by Dave Sargent ; illustrated by
Jane Lenoir.
Prairie Grove, AR. : Ozark Pub., 2000
p. cm.
{Fic}21
1567634613 (CB)
1567634621 (PB)
Selfish Marty Mule's refusal to share his stall with the
other animals results in a fire that threatens Glenda
Goose and her eggs. Includes factual information on
geese.
Geese -- Fiction.
Mules -- Fiction.
Selfishness -- Fiction.
Sharing -- Fiction.
Fires -- Fiction.
Domestic animals -- Fiction.
Lenoir, Jane, 1950- ill.
11864525

Printed in the United States of America

Inspired by

my wish for freedom and protection for the beautiful Canadian Goose and all geese around the world.

Dedicated to

all students who love to watch geese on land, on water and in flight.

Foreword

When Farmer John finds a nest full of goose eggs, he quickly makes Glenda Goose a nest in the hay barn. Glenda is very grateful when her eggs are placed in the new nest and she knows they are safe. Big trouble starts when selfish Marty Mule kicks over the lantern that has been left on a bale of hay. The hay catches on fire and red-hot flames shoot high! The frightened animals run for their lives!

Contents

Glenda Goose

If you would like to have an author of The Feather Tale Series visit your school, free of charge, just call 1-800-321-5671 or 1-800-960-3876.

One

The Electrical Storm

A hot bolt of lightning streaking through the night was followed by a loud clap of thunder. Glenda Goose wriggled her big body into the cozy nest of hay that held her twelve eggs. They were due to hatch any day now, and then she would have twelve little goslings waddling along behind her.

Glenda sighed contentedly. I'm so lucky, she thought. My nest is dry, and I have a good roof over my head. I'm very grateful to Farmer John for making me a nest in this hay barn!

1

The patter of raindrops on the tin roof was soothing. Glenda smiled as she tucked her head beneath one gray and white feathered wing.

"Hey! This is my stall!" a deep voice suddenly yelled. "And I refuse to share it with anybody. You hear? Anybody! Especially a little cat!"

Glenda leaped to her feet.

"Who is fussing so? And why? Something is wrong." she muttered.

"Yeeow!" a kitten complained. "I'm not taking up much room, Marty. Don't be so selfish!"

"I said this is **my** stall," the deep voice thundered, "and you are not welcome to share it!" A bang was followed by a thud, a squall, then a deep chuckle before peace once again descended upon the barn.

"Humph!" Glenda grunted as she settled back down on her nest. "That Marty Mule is going to learn a hard lesson on selfishness one of these days. I had thirteen brothers and sisters, and I learned to share when I was just a little thing. It's not good to be selfish. Not good at all." She cocked her head to one side and listened for several moments before muttering, "The rain has stopped. Maybe Farmer John can harvest his apple crop tomorrow as he planned."

Suddenly the barn door opened, and Farmer John and Molly entered. Farmer John was carrying a lantern. The flame cast a glow of golden light throughout the interior of the barn.

"That was some storm, Molly!" Farmer John said. "Man! I haven't seen lightning like that in some time. It knocked out our electricity, so we'll have to do the chores tonight by the light of the lantern." He chuckled as he added, "It's hard to believe that our folks lived like this every day."

"It really is," Molly agreed. "We take electricity and lights for granted. Why don't I feed the rest of these animals while you get the cows in to be milked," Molly suggested.

"I reckon that's a right good idea, Molly!" Farmer John agreed. "That way, we'll be through with the chores in record time and can rest up for gathering apples tomorrow."

Molly hurried to get feed, and Farmer John set the lantern on a bale of hay near Marty's stall. Glenda watched him put grain and hay in the trough. Then he opened the barn door to let a large calf in for his dinner. Glenda gulped when the little critter ran straight to Marty's feed trough. He pushed Marty Mule aside and started eating the grain. Marty glared and stomped his hoof.

"Uh oh," the big goose groaned. "I have a bad feeling about this!"

"Get away from my trough!" Marty bellowed. "This is my food, and I am not gonna share it!"

The goose hurried to the stall, looked up at the mule, and folded her wings across her breast. She tapped one webbed foot on the barn floor.

"I don't think that Farmer John would appreciate your selfishness, Marty," she hissed.

Marty Mule glared down at her. Then he shifted his gaze to the calf.

"Get out of my feed!" the mule repeated. "Farmer John gave me that feed, and you can't have any of it! And," he said to Glenda, "you get out of my stall, you ornery old goose!"

"It won't hurt you to share a bite or two," Glenda Goose said harshly.

"Look, Marty, it's hard enough for Farmer John and Molly to do the chores without light. They don't need your selfish attitude adding to their problems tonight."

The calf smiled and looked at Marty with big brown eyes as he reached for another bite of grain.

"No!" the mule bellowed again. "I'll not share my feed or my stall!"

Glenda's eyes widened as she saw Marty lift his back foot.

"Marty Mule!" she screamed. "Don't! Don't kick the lantern!"

Two

The Fire

The sound of breaking glass was immediately followed by a yell from Farmer John, a gasp from the goose, and the crackle of fire spreading rapidly over the bale of hay. Suddenly, Molly, carrying some feed, appeared.

Molly's eyes widened in fear as she screamed, "Fire! Oh, no! John! John! Where are you?"

Smoke was beginning to fill the room as flames licked higher and higher above the shattered lantern.

Suddenly Farmer John appeared amid the smoke and flames. He was carrying two buckets of water.

"I'm okay, Molly! You better call the fire department! I'll try to control the flames till they get here!"

As Molly ran toward the house, Farmer John doused the flames with the water. Then he ran back outside to the well to refill his buckets.

"Everybody! Get out!" Glenda yelled. Bandit appeared and helped roll Glenda's eggs out of harm's way.

The calf whirled and took off through the doorway. A sorrel horse, tied in the stall next to Marty Mule, nickered loudly and pawed the ground with his front hoof. Glenda ran to the rope and quickly untied it. The horse whirled and ran outside.

Glenda hurried to the next stall, dodging flames. Marty was standing as though frozen in one spot as the fire inched closer to him. She yelled, "Go, Marty!" When he didn't move, she nipped at his legs with her bill. Then she flapped her feathery wings

and honked as loud as she could.
"Go, Marty! Run for your life!"

The stubborn mule lowered his head and coughed. The barn was full of smoke, but Glenda was able to see a tear streaming down his face.

"I'm staying here," Marty said hoarsely. "It's my fault the barn's on fire. I could never face Farmer John or you and your babies or anybody again because of my selfishness."

The goose stomped her foot and yelled, "We will discuss your selfishness later, Marty Mule. I can't explain right from wrong while my tail feathers are getting singed! Now, come on. Let's get out of here!"

Marty Mule shook his head, and another tear fell upon the barn floor.

Suddenly, Farmer John ran in again. As he tossed both buckets of water on the flames, Glenda heard a dog barking. Barney the Bear Killer was trying to help. He saw that Glenda's eggs had been moved to a safe place, checked the horse stall, then stopped at Marty's stall.

"Marty won't leave, Barney!" Glenda yelled. "What can we do?"

Barney the Bear Killer looked at Marty, and the stubborn ole mule shook his head.

Barney glanced at Glenda, then gave Marty a hard look. He showed his teeth and growled a deep growl. He leaped and grabbed the stubborn mule's halter in his long, sharp teeth. He growled again and slowly began inching his way backward. Like it or not, he was dragging ole Marty Mule toward the barn door. Glenda Goose did her part. She followed, honking and flapping her big, feathery wings every step of the way.

As the dog, mule and goose left the barn, Farmer John ran past them with more buckets of water.

A moment later, Glenda saw the yard light come on. The glow looked normal to the goose.

"Good," she said to Barney and Marty. "The electricity is on again. Maybe things will get back to normal around here." Then she heard the sirens from the fire trucks blaring in the distance. "Or not," she mumbled.

Within moments, flashing red lights streaked up the lane. Glenda heard someone behind her. She turned and saw that Farmer John and Molly were standing beside Marty and both were patting Barney on the head. To her surprise, Farmer John was smiling! Glenda tapped Marty on the leg with one wing.

"Pssst, Marty," she whispered. "Look at Farmer John."

But the stubborn mule would not look. He just shook his head and walked into the darkness of the night.

When the fire truck stopped, Farmer John hurried out to talk to the firemen.

"Boys," he said, as he wiped his face, "I sure appreciate you coming out here, but thankfully, I got the fire out before it burned the barn down."

Glenda Goose breathed a sigh of relief before running to catch up with Marty.

"Wait, Marty Mule," she called. "Everything is okay. The fire is out. Nobody was hurt."

Marty Mule stopped and turned around.

"What do you mean 'the fire is out'?" he asked.

"It's true. Farmer John put the fire out. And," she gasped as she stopped beside him, "no permanent damage was done, Marty."

"And, what do you mean 'no damage was done'?" he said hoarsely. "The horse ran away, the cows wasn't milked, that hungry calf wasn't fed, Farmer John ran his poor legs off carrying water, and the hay barn almost burned down." He sighed.

Again, the mule began walking slowly toward the woods.

"Wait, Marty," Glenda pleaded. "Where are you going?"

"It doesn't matter," he muttered. "I'm a troublemaker, and I'm gonna run away. Goodbye, Glenda Goose. I won't be coming back here to Farmer John's place ever again."

Suddenly, Glenda honked and ran after him.

"Wait, Marty Mule!" she yelled. "Wait for me. I have a plan that will make it all okay again. Listen . . ."

Three

Doing the Right Thing

The Rhode Island Red rooster was crowing as Farmer John and Molly left the house. Glenda saw Farmer John go into the tool shed and return with a saw and ladder.

"Molly," he said, "if you'll get the hammer and nails, we can start the repairs on the burned-out stall."

Molly hurried inside and got the requested items.

"We should be getting our apple crop gathered today," he said sadly, "but these repairs have to be done."

Molly gave him a couple of pats on the shoulder and smiled.

"This won't take long, John," she said quietly. "And then I'll help you with the apples."

He smiled and winked at her as he murmured, "You're a good wife, Molly. Let's go to work."

Glenda breathed a sigh of relief as she watched them enter the barn. Seconds later, she was running toward the apple orchard as fast as her short legs could carry her.

A short time later, she saw Marty Mule. He was standing beside dozens of burlap bags that were full to the top with ripe, red, juicy apples. Glenda smiled when she saw the early morning sunlight dancing upon the happy face of the tired but very proud mule.

"Well, I did it," he said quietly. "All of the apples have been gathered from the trees, and I didn't bruise even one of them with my teeth."

"This is wonderful, Marty!" the goose said. She patted him gently on the knee with one wing and winked.

"I knew you could do it," she murmured. "I am very proud of you. But," Glenda added, "not as grateful and proud as Farmer John will be!"

"I feel good about my work," Marty agreed. "And I feel good in my heart. I'll never be selfish again, Glenda Goose. I promise."

Glenda smiled and nodded before slowly turning back toward the barnyard. She wanted to roll her eggs back into her nest. Of course, if the fire had burned her nest, she would have to make a new one. Well, at least Bandit had helped her move her eggs. She was grateful to him for that. Glenda always had lots of friends because she was always nice and polite to others.

"Yes," Glenda mumbled as she walked toward the hay barn. "That Marty Mule did a real fine job. And I believe he has learned a lesson on selfishness that he won't soon forget. Unless . . . oh . . . that mule does have a healthy appetite. No. He will share if the need arises. Won't he? And surely he won't eat those apples. Will he? Hmmm . . .

Four

Goose Facts

Goose is a common name for a number of species of water birds of the same family as ducks and swans. When applied to individual birds, the word *goose* strictly speaking, refers to the female, the male is called gander. Only the word *goose,* however, is used in the names of species.

Several groups of waterfowl, all generally larger than ducks and smaller than swans, have been called geese. The so-called true geese belong to three genera. These are birds of the northern hemisphere, nesting in arctic and temperate areas. Most are strongly migratory but are able to winter as far north as Alaska and New England.

In North America the best-known and most widely distributed species is the Canadian goose. Its length ranges from 25 to 45 inches. The tail, head, and neck is black with a white patch on the cheek, and the body some shade of brown.

CANADA GOOSE

The Canada goose has also been introduced in both Scandinavia and Great Britain. Its nesting grounds range from arctic Canada and Alaska to the prairie states of the United States. Its color and size is like that of the North America Canada goose.

Similar in size to the smallest Canadian geese is the brant, which nests in the Arctic and winters chiefly on salt water.

BRANT GOOSE

Also nesting in the Arctic are two white species, the snow goose and the smaller Ross's goose.

SNOW GOOSE   BLUE GOOSE

ROSS'S GOOSE

The blue goose, a bluish-gray bird with a white head, was long thought to be a separate species but is now known to be a color phase of the snow goose.

RED-BREASTED GOOSE

BARNACLE GOOSE

GREYLAG

NE-NE

SPUR-WINGED GOOSE

The ne-ne, a terrestrial goose endemic to Hawaii and the state's emblem, was saved from extinction through breeding in captivity.

Among the true geese of Eurasia, the greylag is the ancestor of most breeds of domestic geese; the Chinese goose is an exception, being a heavyset descendant of the slender swan goose of Asia.

A number of breeds of geese are raised domestically. Among the most important domestic geese are the Toulouse goose, an all-gray breed originating in France; the Embden, an all-white goose originating in

Germany; and the African, a tall, gray goose that fattens more rapidly than any other breed. Both the flesh and the eggs of geese are eaten. Geese are the source of the delicacy, pâté de foie gras, made from goose livers that are abnormally enlarged by overfeeding the geese and then depriving them of exercise. Domestic geese are also commercially valuable for their feathers, which are used in pillows, insulated clothing, and sleeping bags.

Not closely related to the true geese are several waterfowl that share the common name. These include the primitive magpie goose of Australia, with strong toes that are only partially webbed, and the sheldgeese of the Falkland Islands and the south part of South America.

Sheldgeese differ from true geese in that the sexes may be quite different in their coloration.

Scientific classification: Geese belong to the family *Anatidae,* of the order *Anseriformes.* True geese belong to the genera *Anser, Branta,* and *Chen.* The Canada goose is classified as *Branta canadensis*, and the brant as *Branta bernicla.* The snow goose is classified as *Chen caerulescens*, and Ross's goose as *Chen rossii*, although both are often placed in the genus *Anser.* The ne-ne is classified as *Branta sandricensis.* The greylag is classified as *Anser anser*, and the swan goose as *Anser cygnoides.* The magpie goose is classified as *Anseranas semipalmata.* Sheldgeese make up the genus *Chloephaga.*